D1549936

Tips for Reading Together

Children learn best when reading is fun.

- Talk about the title and the pictures on the cover.
- Look through the pictures together and discuss what you think the story might be about.
- Read the story together, inviting your child to read as much of it as they can.
- Give lots of praise as your child reads, and help them when necessary.
- Try different ways of helping if they get stuck on a word. For example, get them to say the first sound of the word, or break it into chunks, or read the whole sentence again, trying to guess the word. Focus on the meaning.
- Have fun finding the hidden letter shapes.
- Re-read the story later, encouraging your child to read as much of it as they can.

Children enjoy re-reading stories and this helps to build their confidence.

Have fun!

Find the letter shapes in the pictures that spell out the word SNOWBALL

Husky Adventure

Roderick Hunt • Alex Brychta

OXFORD

UNIVERSITY PRESS

It had been snowing. Kipper
wanted Floppy to pull his sled.
"Go on, Floppy! Pull!" he called.

Floppy didn't want to pull
the sled. He ran and hid in
Biff's bedroom.

Suddenly, the magic key began
to glow. It took Floppy into
an adventure.

The magic took Floppy to a
dark, cold forest. There was
snow everywhere.

The snow felt cold on Floppy's
paws and a cold wind was blowing.
"Brrrr!" thought Floppy.

Floppy began to walk, but his
paws sank in the deep snow.

He heard a howling sound.
AOOOOOW!
"What is that?" thought Floppy.

Oh no! It was a pack of wolves.
They had red eyes and long white
teeth. They growled at Floppy.

Floppy was scared of the wolves.
He ran through the trees.

Suddenly, Floppy fell down.
He rolled over and over. He went
faster and faster.

Then he hit a tree.
BUMP!

Floppy lay in the snow with his eyes shut.

A man ran up.

"Quick!" he said. "My boy is sick.
I must get him to hospital. I need
another dog to pull the sled."

The man took Floppy to the sled.
"Oh no!" thought Floppy.
"Another pack of wolves!"

But they were not wolves, they
were husky dogs. The dogs growled.
"Are you the new dog? You look
too floppy to pull a sled," they said.

The man put straps on Floppy.
"You've got to run fast," he said.
"We must get to the hospital."

The biggest dog barked at Floppy. "Just keep up, you floppy dog," he said. "We've got to run fast."

Floppy was cross. "Don't call
me a floppy dog," he said. "I'll
show you!"

The sled went faster and faster.
"Slow down!" panted the husky
dogs. "We can't keep up with you."

At last, they got to the hospital.

"Thank you!" shouted the man.

"You've saved my son."

The husky dogs looked at Floppy. "Wow! You can run fast!" they said. "You're not a floppy dog."

"You can stay with us," said
the husky dogs. "We need a dog
like you."

The magic key began to glow.
"Good!" thought Floppy. "I need
a rest."

"Come and pull my sled, Floppy,"
said Kipper.

"Oh no!" thought Floppy.

Think about the story

Why did Floppy go and hide?

Did the Huskies think Floppy would be good at pulling the sled? Why not?

Why couldn't the man take his son to hospital in a car?

Where would you like to go on a magic key adventure?

A Maze

Help the dog team to find their way to the hospital.

More books for you to enjoy

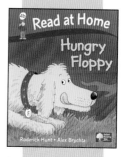

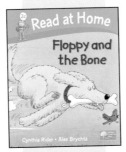

Level 1: Getting Ready

Level 2: Starting to Read

Level 3: Becoming a Reader

Level 4: Building Confidence

OXFORD
UNIVERSITY PRESS

Great Clarendon Street,
Oxford OX2 6DP

Text © Roderick Hunt
Illustrations © Alex Brychta 2005
Designed by Andy Wilson

First published 2005

ISBN 0 19 838564 1

10 9 8 7 6 5 4 3 2 1

Printed in China by Imago